Cursed

A Yorkshire Ghost Short Story

(Ghosts of Thores-Cross, book 2)

By

Karen Perkins

LionheART Publishing House

First published in Great Britain in 2014 by

LionheART Publishing House

LionheART Publishing House
Harrogate

www.lionheartgalleries.co.uk

www.facebook.com/lionheartpublishing

lionheartpublishinghouse@gmail.com

Cover Design by CC Morgan Creative Visuals

Prologue

Thruscross, North Yorkshire

7th August 1966 – 11:30 a.m.

'Right, tea break over, lads, back to work. Rog, Steve, you're up on Hanging Moor in the bulldozers. As soon as they've gone through, Paul and Simon, you get the chippings down. And take care – don't go past the markers, that drop's lethal.'

The road crew groaned, threw their dregs of tea to the ground and refastened their flasks before clambering into their machines to dig out the access road to the new dam spanning the Washburn Valley. The valley would be flooded in a month's time, creating the new reservoir for the Leeds Corporation Waterworks to supply half of Leeds with drinking water, and the road should have been completed last month.

Rog led the way, the large bucket scraping heather and peat, then dumping it into the waiting tipper truck.

Steve followed, making a deeper cut. Together they

gouged an ugly scar over the pristine Yorkshire moorland.

'Bugger,' Steve cried out and jolted in his seat, knocking the control levers. The big digger wobbled, teetered, then slowly toppled over towards the edge and a sheer wooded drop of a hundred and fifty feet to the valley bottom below.

'Steve!' Rog cried. 'Lads, help!'

The rest of the crew downed tools and diggers and rushed to the stricken bulldozer. By the time they reached it, Rog was already clambering on to the cab, desperately trying not to look at the vista that opened up before him only a few feet away.

'Steve?' he called again. No answer. His mate lay unconscious, twisted in his seat. 'Bugger!' The digger slid a foot or two in the wrong direction.

'Rog, get down; she's going over!' Andy, the foreman, shouted.

'No – Steve's out cold.'

'You're no help to him if your weight pushes it over the edge – get down! We'll get help, but we need to secure the digger somehow, keep her steady.'

Rog took a last look at his mate then nodded. He realised he couldn't get into the cab without destabilising the digger further and he had no idea how serious Steve's injuries were. He climbed down carefully, just as Simon drew up in the tipper truck. Half full of soil and rock, it was the heaviest vehicle there.

Andy got on the radio to inform his boss at the dam where there was a telephone to call for help, while Paul ran over with a chain. He secured it round one of the digging arms, and Simon backed up – slowly – until the chain was taut.

The digger shifted, turning around the pivot point they'd created. The back end now hung off the edge of the cliff.

'Keep it there, Simon,' Andy called. 'And keep it in reverse – if the edge fails, you'll need to pull him backwards.'

'Can't he just do that anyway?' Rog asked.

'We don't know how badly he's hurt. If he's broken his back or neck, moving him could make it worse. We don't want to move him unless we have to – not until the Fire Brigade and ambulance get here. What happened anyway?'

'Uh.' Rog pulled his attention away from the downed machine. 'I don't know – he shouted out, then rolled it.'

'He shouted *before* he rolled?'

'Yes.'

'Andy, Rog. Come and have a look at this,' Paul called and beckoned them over to join him where Steve had made his last cut.

'What is it?' Andy came hurrying over.

'Uh, looks like a skull.'

'What? Oh Christ, it's a bloody skeleton! Well, that's us finished, lads, no more work here for at least a month while they sort this one out,' Rog said.

'Forget that, we'll just go round it,' Andy said.

The three men looked over at Steve, then back into the grave. Only the skull and shoulder girdle were visible. As one, they shuddered as a worm pushed its way out of the compacted earth behind the jaw bones, for a moment looking as if the skull had stuck an emaciated tongue out at them.

Rebirth

7ᵗʰ August 1966 – 7:00 p.m.

John Ramsgill rushed through the door to the Stonehouse Inn and over to the corner table by the log fire where his mother – Old Ma Ramsgill – was usually to be found at this time in the evening with a pint of stout before her.

'Ma, have you heard the news?'

'Aye, it's all these fools can talk about,' she said gruffly. No one took offence; Old Ma Ramsgill had been a regular in this pub since before most of them had been born. She called everyone 'fool', and everyone called her 'Old Ma Ramsgill', although never to her face. To her face she was 'Ma' to the whole moor, although the moor was vastly depleted now. The families who'd lived down the hill for generations had moved away over the last few years to make way for the reservoir.

'Who do you think it is?'

'Who?'

'The skeleton, Ma!' John bit back his frustration at his mother's obdurate nature. At thirty two he should be used to it, but she could still flare his impatience with a single word.

He took a deep breath and used a calmer tone. 'The skeleton they found up on Hanging Moor – where the old drovers' roads cross.'

She looked up at her son, for the first time showing interest. 'Where the ways cross? Bugger.' She said no more and again John fought to restrain his frustration.

'What do you mean, Ma? Why "Bugger"?'

'It's Jennet, she'll have been woken.'

'Jennet? What, you mean the witch? But she's just a story, she's not real.'

'Oh, she's real all right, lad.'

John turned to greet Wilf Moore as he sat to join Ma. He was almost as old – and as stubborn – as his mother, not to anyone's surprise: they were distant cousins.

'She's the reason thee's the only Ramsgill in these parts – by birth, anyroad.'

'Apart from the bairns,' Old Ma Ramsgill put in.

'Aye, apart from the bairns.' Wilf paused. 'Keep an eye on them, lad. If Jennet's awake, they ain't safe.'

'What? What are you talking about? Why would my children be in danger because an old skeleton's been dug up?'

Ma and Wilf looked at each other. 'Not here, lad, not in t' pub. We'll talk tomorrow, early. Sue too, she needs to hear it.'

John opened his mouth to say more, but Ma held up her hand, drained half her stout and said, 'Best get me another of these, John. One for Wilf too. We'll need as much fortification as we can muster.'

John sighed in exasperation and went to the bar. He knew from long experience that he would get no more from his mother – not until she was ready to talk.

8th August 1966 – 3:00 a.m.

Old Ma Ramsgill dragged herself out of sleep, sweating and gasping for breath. She fumbled at her bedside table to switch the light on, found her glasses, and peered at the carriage clock she'd inherited from Grandma Moore. Three o'clock. The time restless spirits were at their strongest.

She reached a trembling hand for a glass of water and knocked it over. 'Buggeration!' she exclaimed. Then she said it again and again, louder each time. She held her head in her hands and wept. Something she hadn't done for many a long year. Only one thing could make her weep after all she'd seen in life: family. And her family was in grave danger. She just had to make them realise it, then she had a chance of keeping them safe.

She threw the blankets back and eased herself out of bed. Her slippers were wet, but that was still better than barefoot on three-o'clock-chilled flagstones. Shuffling to the kitchen, she cursed again.

She filled the kettle and set it on the AGA – not one of those fancy new ones, but one that had been in this house almost as long as she had.

'Uh.' She bent double, hanging on to the edge of the range as images from her nightmare flashed through her mind. Dark grey clouds morphing into the face of a woman, hair flowing round an expression of sheer hatred and rage.

A wolf bounding across the moorland. Instead of taking a lamb, it snatched an infant from its pushchair.

Fire consuming not the house she stood in, Gate House, which had been in the Ramsgill family for centuries, but Wolf Farm. The farm her son, John, was talking about renovating as soon as he could save up enough cash. *Or as soon as I snuff it and he gets his hands on the Ramsgill land.* Screams of terror echoed through her head. The screams of her family.

Still no let up. Villagers drowning in the river. Babies thrown on to fires. The rocking stone grinding a sinister soundtrack to it all.

The screech of the kettle broke the spell and Old Ma Ramsgill shook her head, wincing at a sudden pain in her temple, and poured the water into her mother's old earthenware teapot.

'Dreams, just dreams,' she muttered to herself. 'That stone ain't moved for years – not like when I was a girl and a storm could set it going.'

She poured out the tea, threw in four sugar cubes, and sipped, wincing again as she burnt her lip.

'Stupid old woman,' she mocked herself. 'Get a grip, thee'll need all thy faculties to take on that witch.'

8th August 1966 – 10:00 a.m.

'About time,' Old Ma Ramsgill scolded her son and daughter-in-law when they arrived.

'We came as soon as we could,' John said. 'I had the milking to do and Sue had to feed the little ones and get Richie off to school.'

'What? Thee's never sent the boy to school? Thee fool. Thee can't let him out of thy sight!'

Sue scowled at her mother-in-law. 'It's the law, Ma, he's six, he has to go to school.'

'Tell them he's sick. This is more important.'

'What? An old skeleton. Dead. How can that be a threat?'

Ma sighed. 'Thee don't understand. Go through, I'll make another pot then tell thee the tale.'

Sue glanced at John, who shrugged. She thanked her lucky stars once again that she'd persuaded John to move away from Gate House to one of the new cottages built near the Stonehouse to provide accommodation for those forced out of their soon-to-be-flooded homes, even though he still worked the Ramsgill farm. She was still trying to persuade him out of buying that old ruined farmhouse. A couple of hundred yards up the lane from Old Ma Ramsgill was far too close for comfort; or peace.

John reached into the pram to lift the twins out, but Sue stopped him. 'Let them sleep, John, they've been up half the night.'

'And so have you.' He embraced his wife and kissed her forehead. 'They'll sleep through before long.'

'Can't come soon enough,' Sue said and led the way to the front room.

John followed, carrying the tea tray.

'Just move them journals out the way, lass.'

Sue did as Ma bid, piling the old, leather-bound books to one side of the coffee table so John could put the tray down. Her interest was piqued by them, but after seven years of being a Ramsgill, she knew better than to push Ma into an explanation.

'Thee pour, lass,' Ma said as she sank into her armchair. Sue looked at her in surprise. Old Ma Ramsgill never let anyone else pour the tea in her house. She always had to be mother.

'You all right, Ma?' John asked.

'Just a bit tired, Son. Bad night.'

'Your hip playing up again?'

'No, nowt like that.' She took a deep breath. 'It were Jennet.'

'What do you mean?' John asked at the same time as Sue's, 'Who's Jennet?'

'Thee's not told her, John?'

He shrugged. 'Why? It's just an old story, scared me silly as a lad when you talked about her. I'll not inflict that on my kids.'

Ma ignored the jibe. 'It ain't a story, Son, and I'm surprised thy mother didn't tell thee either, lass. Jennet's real. She lived in this valley 'bout two hundred years ago – in Wolf Farm as a matter of fact.'

John looked sceptical and Sue sipped her tea, unsure what was going on.

'She was treated bad by Ramsgills. Turned her rotten, our ancestors did.'

'You said she was a witch.'

'Aye, cunning woman they were called then. Healers.'

'What, like a herbalist?' Sue asked.

'Aye, summat like that. Anyroad, she became a pariah—'

'Why?'

'Had an affair with a married man.'

'A Ramsgill?'

'John, stop interrupting. Let me tell the story.'

'Sorry, Ma.'

'But yes, with a Ramsgill. Owned most of the valley then, Ramsgills did. An important family in these parts. Anyroad, back to Jennet. Folk didn't take kindly to that sort of behaviour – not like nowadays where everyone seems to be at it. They shunned her.'

'What, everyone?'

Ma glared at Sue, then her expression softened. 'Most

everyone. One kept her company, an ancestor of thine, lass, Mary Farmer, that's why I'm surprised thee ain't heard of her. But it weren't enough.' She tapped the pile of journals.

'It's all in here. Couldn't cope, couldn't Jennet. Bitter she was, it twisted her. She stopped healing, started cursing. Cursed this whole valley. Look, let me show thee.'

She shuffled the pile of books until she found the one she wanted, turned the pages, then handed it to John. 'Read that.'

John glanced at Sue, then his mother, and decided to humour her. ' "Aye, that's right. Witch!" she screamed at us all. "And how many of thee's drunk my potions? Whispered my spells? How can thee be sure they were to heal, or for love? Which of thee men can be sure thy woman ain't snuck a 'love potion' in thy ale? Everyone here's cursed by my hands!" '

'Her last words, them was. She also cursed the valley, the village, and the Ramsgills in particular. Look at that bloody great dam they're building. The whole village will be drowned by end of year. Gone. Just like she said.'

'But that's just coincidence, surely,' Sue interrupted. 'Given long enough, predictions are bound to come true. It's been two hundred years, I hardly think you can blame a new reservoir in 1966 on a girl who lived in the 1700s.'

'I thought thee might say that, lass, so I drew this up while I were waiting.' Old Ma Ramsgill passed over a sheet of paper. 'It's the Ramsgill family tree going back to Jennet's time.'

'What are we looking for?' Sue asked.

'Look at the children,' Ma told her. 'See how many die? "Only one may live to carry the curse to the next generation, then they will suffer their losses." She said *that* about the Ramsgills an'all.'

The silence that followed was broken by a cry from the kitchen.

'That's Jayne,' Sue said. 'Robert will wake any second now.' Her words were accompanied by a second wailing and both parents stood to retrieve their children.

'Do you believe any of this, John?' Sue asked in a whisper.

'No, but . . .' John held Robert high and planted a kiss on the crown of his head, breathing in his milky baby smell.

'But what? It's nonsense. Witches don't exist – not in the way Ma means. And neither do curses.'

'But the family tree?'

'It goes back centuries, how do we know it's accurate? Ma's going daft, John. She's nearly eighty, living alone in this creepy old house, the whole valley about to change with this reservoir. No wonder she's seeing witches and curses. Thruscross is not haunted by a two-hundred-year-old ghost.'

'It'll do no harm to listen to her, Sue. There are things out there we don't understand.'

'You *believe* her?'

John shrugged. 'Not really but she's never steered me wrong yet, even pushing me to pop the question to you. Deep down . . . I don't know. Deep down I can't just dismiss it.'

Sue didn't reply, just raised her eyebrows and pulled in a sharp breath. She turned and went back to the living room.

'I might be nearly eighty, lass, but there's nowt wrong with me hearing.'

Sue flushed and stared at the floor.

'Aye, might be daft an'all – there's plenty round here who'd attest to that. But senile I'm not. This is real, and the sooner thee accepts that, the safer them bairns will be. Mark me words – when Jennet wakes, Ramsgills die. She was disturbed yesterday by them damn fool diggers. Taken blood too. None of us are safe.'

Relive

9th August 1966 – 7:00 am

'John, wake up, you're having a nightmare.' Sue shook her husband awake.

'Wha—? Huh? Oh, thank God.'

'You were thrashing around like anything – what were you dreaming about?'

John sat up and ran his hands over his face and through his hair. 'God, it was awful. I dreamed of that witch, Jennet. She burned the twins. God.' He shuddered. 'I'm never going to get that image out of my mind. And the smell. Christ!'

'Smell? In a dream?'

John shrugged. 'It was a vivid one. Too vivid. What time is it, anyway?'

'Bloody hell, seven o'clock, the twins have slept through!'

'Hallelujah. Well, that's something.'

'I'll go check on them,' Sue said, getting out of bed and shrugging on her robe. 'God, a full night's sleep, I feel like a new woman.'

John didn't reply, his head was in his hands again.

'John! John! Oh God, no!'

He jumped out of bed and ran into the twins' room.

Sue held Jayne in her arms, tears pouring down her face. 'They're – they're cold, John, they're cold. Ring 999.'

Disbelieving, John ran to the crib and picked Robert up. His little body was stiff. Sobbing, John looked at his wife and struggled to get his words out. 'Ma was right. It's Jennet. She's back.'

14th August 1966 – 4:00 p.m.

'We have to protect Richie,' Old Ma Ramsgill insisted. 'Send him away, far enough away that he's out of reach.'

'Not now, Ma, please. It's the twins' wake. Let us say goodbye to them properly.'

'There's no time, thee fool,' Ma shouted, bringing a silence down on the Stonehouse. She took a deep breath. 'Jennet won't respect our grief. She'll come for thee or Richie next, John. Thee's the only ones with Ramsgill blood.'

'Oh not your bloody ghost again, Ma,' Tom Grange said, then laughed.

'Still thy tongue, boy.' Wilf jumped to Ma's defence. 'Thee knows better than to speak to thy elders like that. And thee'd do well to heed Ma's words. All of thee would,' he added, his voice rising.

Ma took over. 'The whole valley's in trouble, not just Ramsgills – she cursed us all, don't forget. All of thy ancestors played a part in her story. I know it sounds like a fairy story to thee young 'uns, but this is real. This is Yorkshire, it's full of bloody ghosts and this one's a devil.'

Someone sniggered.

'Sarah Wainwright, I might have guessed. Thy ma were just as flighty as thee is.'

'Don't you talk about my ma, she ain't well.'

'Aye, soft in the head, and thee knows why? She saw Jennet the last time she woke, when she took my Jack. Ask her, go on, ask her. Helped me put Jennet back to rest she did and it broke her.'

Sarah was in tears. 'You evil old . . . *cow*,' she spat at Ma. 'You know nothing about my ma, nothing!'

'I've known her all her life, stupid girl. Know her better than thee does, I'll bet.'

Sarah screamed and dropped her glass, then pointed at the door.

'What? What is it, lass?'

'A-a-a woman . . .'

'Where?'

'The doorway. Can't you see her? Can't *anyone* see her? She's laughing at us!' Sarah's voice rose in hysteria.

'Buggeration,' Old Ma Ramsgill said and put herself between the door and the frightened girl. 'Get gone, Jennet Scot. Thee's done enough, leave us be.'

Everyone heard the laugh, then silence reigned once again. Sue nudged John and showed him her arm – raised in goosebumps. 'It's freezing in here.'

'I know.'

'Anyone else think I'm an evil old cow? No? Just as well. Get thyselves home, hang rosemary at thy doors and windows and sprinkle salt at every entrance. Oh, and pray to whatever god thee believes in – we're going to need them all.'

15th August 1966 – 6:00 a.m.

John opened his front door only to be pushed aside by Old Ma Ramsgill.

'Sarah Wainwright's dead. They're saying she was mauled by a dog. It weren't a dog, it were Jennet.'

'Wha—? Ma, no, tell me you're joking.'

'Why the bloody hell would I joke about summat like that? Damn fool boy.'

'But-but how do you know it's Jennet?'

'She used to appear as a barguest – an evil spirit disguised as an animal. Jennet's a black dog. She's up to her old tricks, and it don't look like she's happy to restrict herself just to our family. Get dressed, get Sue and Richie, and get thyselves to Gate House. We need to stop her.'

'How? How the bloody hell can we stop a two-hundred-year-old witch?' Sue asked from the doorway. 'From what you said last night at the wake, you've already tried once, yet she's back.'

'Aye. But we kept her spirit bound to her bones for near on thirty year. She'd still be sleeping if not for that bloody dam.'

'So we can do it again?'

Old Ma Ramsgill said nothing.

'Ma?' John prompted. 'Can we do it again?'

Ma took a deep breath, then heaved a great sigh. 'No. They'll be taking the bloody bones, if they haven't done already. They're no good to us now.'

'So what are we going to do?'

For the first time in many years, Old Ma Ramsgill looked her age. 'I don't know, Son. But we'd better damn well come up with something quick or this is only the start.'

7:00 a.m.

'This is my journal. The one I started last time,' Ma said. 'Thee read it out, John, my eyes ain't what they were. Then we'll go through the others, see what else our ancestors did.' She passed the journal to her son and a piece of paper slipped out. The family tree.

Sue picked it up and opened it out. 'All the twins,' she said. 'They all died together.' She passed the diagram to John and they studied it, their tears mingling amidst the names of John's ancestors, smudging the ink.

'Take care of that,' Old Ma Ramsgill snapped. 'Richie may need it one day – or his kids.'

'Not if we stop her,' John said, the emotion making his words crack, but the purpose and intent in his voice was still clear.

'Ramsgills have been trying to do that for two centuries, John. Yet still she's here. We'll do everything we can, but it may not be enough. When I'm gone, thee'll have to prepare Richie. Make sure he believes it.'

They sat with their own thoughts for a while as the implications of failure sank in, only the radio breaking the silence.

'Today's headlines. Two people died last night after being mauled by dogs. Adam Carter from Harrogate and Sarah Wainwright from Thruscross.'

All three Ramsgills listened in growing horror.

'Who's Adam Carter?' John asked.

'Shh,' Ma said. 'Listen.'

'Witnesses to both attacks describe the same vicious dog, despite the attacks being fifteen miles apart.

'A spokesperson for the North Yorkshire Police has

urged local residents to be vigilant and report any sightings of a large unaccompanied black dog to them. Under no circumstances should the animal be approached.

'In other news . . .'

'Who's Adam Carter?' John asked again. 'What does he have to do with this?'

'Give me that family tree,' Ma snapped. 'Yes, look – at Jennet's time, Richard Ramsgill was married to Elizabeth Cartwright. It's my bet he's a descendant of that family.'

'Harrogate,' Sue said. 'He was killed in *Harrogate*, not Thruscross. I thought you said she only killed here.'

Ma stared at the journals. 'She's only killed here before. But then her bones were undisturbed. Either she's so angry at her grave being dug up that it's given her the energy to travel further, or her bones are in Harrogate.'

'No, they've got archaeologists and all sorts up there, *brushing* the bloody peat off the bones.'

'Then who knows how far she can go?' said Sue. 'Where can we send Richie if Jennet can find him wherever he is? Mary Hornwright from down the hill moved to Harrogate, we were going to send him to stay with her, but it isn't safe is it? It isn't safe anywhere.'

'Shh, listen.' Old Ma Ramsgill pointed at the radio.

'In preparation for the opening of the new reservoir in the Washburn Valley, Thruscross Dam has already been closed to perform a test flood. The water should be at the expected level of the final reservoir in the next few days.'

The Ramsgills stared at the radio, all thinking the same thing. *How will Jennet react to that?*

'Oh! What's that?' Sue jumped to her feet at the sound of a horn, but John beat her to the window.

'Fire engine and ambulance. They're heading to the dam. Must have been another accident.'

Silence.

It was broken by Sue, who almost whispered, 'John, do you see her?'

'Who?'

'That woman. On the edge of the wood. Staring at the house.'

'Where?'

'What does she look like?' Old Ma Ramsgill asked, joining them at the window.

'Young, long dark hair, a bit wild. Dressed in, I don't know, a wool skirt? It's plain anyway, dowdy. And she's clutching a shawl around herself.'

'That's her.'

Sue and John stared at Ma.

'We have no time to waste. She's coming after thee next. Either that or Richie.'

'She's smiling,' Sue said. 'Waving. Now she's gone. What does that mean? Why did she wave? She looked almost – friendly.'

'Let's hope she recognised thee.'

'Recognised her – what do you mean, Ma?' John asked.

'Remember I told thee last week – the only one in the village that didn't shun her were Mary Farmer. Thy great-great-great . . . Bugger it. Thy ancestor, Sue.'

'So am I safe?'

Old Ma Ramsgill shrugged. 'Who knows? She might have been mocking thee, but thee've a better chance than the rest of us, lass.'

'Does that mean Richie's safe too?'

Ma stared out the window. 'Doubt it, lass. He may have Farmer blood, but he's also a Ramsgill, and he bears the name of the one she hates most.'

A banging on the door made them all jump. John went to answer it. He came back into the room with Wilf.

'I've seen her, Ma, I've seen her. So's the Stockdale girl.'

'So have I,' said Sue.

'She's going to kill the whole damn lot of us,' Wilf said, sinking down on to the sofa.

'Not if I can help it,' Ma said and shuffled back to her armchair. 'But we're going to have to move quick.'

'What can we do? Her bones will soon be gone, and anyway, we can't get near them. We can't bind her to them as you did before,' Sue said, her fear evident in her strident voice.

'The reservoir,' John said from the window. 'It's already filling, if we bind her to one of those buildings, she'll be under the water and can do no harm.'

'Aye, that might work, Son.'

'But which building? What has the strongest connection to her?'

'The church,' Ma said. 'She hated it, as it did her. And it'll be the strongest protection.'

'Can thee do it, though? Can thee stop her, Ma?' Wilf asked.

'I bloody well hope so, but I don't know, Wilf. I don't know. She's stronger this time and I'm old. Old and tired. But I can tell thee one thing – I'll have a damned good go at it, thee see if I don't.'

Return

15th August 1966 – 7:00 p.m.

Sue opened the door to the cottage to let Ma in. 'God, what an awful night,' she said as her mother-in-law entered.

'God has nowt to do with it, lass. This is Jennet. Good to see thee's nailed horseshoes on the door, at least thee's listening now. Has thee a fire lit?'

'Yes, come through.'

Ma sat in the chair nearest the fire and held her hands and feet to the heat. 'A glass of stout wouldn't go amiss.'

'Here you are, Ma, all ready for you,' John said, offering a pint of Samuel Smith's Oatmeal Stout to his mother. 'Got special supplies in from the Stonehouse.'

'Good, I'm going to need it.'

'Are you sure you wouldn't be more comfortable at Gate House?'

'Don't be a fool, boy, she knows it too well, it's the first place Jennet will look for me when she realises what we're up to. Did thee get the stone from Wolf Farm?'

'Here.' John picked up the stone he'd prised loose

from the hearth of Jennet's old home. 'Ma . . .'

'What, Son?' Ma waited. 'Spit it out, what's up?'

'Have you seen the water level?'

'Aye.'

'Well, what do we do?'

'What does thee think thee bloody does? Swim.'

All three jumped at a flash of lightning and immediate thunderclap.

Ma relaxed into her chair and sipped her stout.

'Ma?'

'Give me a minute, Son.' She closed her eyes. 'Aye, she's strong all right. This storm? It's her. She's watching the valley flood and she loves it. Her curse is coming to pass.' Ma opened her eyes. 'We have to do this now, while she's distracted. Any news from Wilf or Stockdales?'

'Haven't heard anything.'

'Good. We'd know if either had been harmed. She's forgotten about them – at least for the moment. We can't waste any time. Pass me my bag, Son. And get ready with that hearthstone.'

John passed her the rucksack and she pulled out a canvas drawstring bag, then the journals.

'Do you really need all of those?'

'Hope not, Son. But better to have 'em. Just in case.'

John nodded.

'Right, thee two, both ready?'

John and Sue nodded.

'Where's nipper?'

'With my sister in York,' Sue replied.

Ma nodded. 'Let's hope that's far enough. At least we know she's here.'

'Stand by with that stone. I'll tell thee when I'm

ready.' Ma heaved herself to her feet and stood directly in front of the fire, bracing herself against the stone wall before she stood straight and opened her canvas bag.

She pulled out a cloth figure.

'What the hell's that, Ma?'

'A poppet. It's filled with moors' peat and heather.'

'Is that supposed to be Jennet?' Sue asked.

'It's supposed to represent her.'

'How? It's just a doll, and a bloody rough one at that,' John said.

'Did thee not hear me? It *represents* her. It has the earth of her home and a slip of paper with her name and family history inside. Now, is thee going to ask me for a lesson or let me get on with this and save thy son?'

No answer.

'Right then, glad we've got that sorted, now hush while I do this.'

She glared at her son and daughter-in-law then, satisfied, took a deep breath and held the poppet out before her.

'Woman of cloth thee is now.

'Woman of flesh and blood thee once were.

'I name thee Jennet Scot.

'No more shall thee do me and mine wrong.

'Never again shall thee take the life of a Ramsgill.

'By the power of the gods, my will and that of the Ramsgills I command this.'

She threw the poppet on to the fire and John and Sue jumped back at the flare of flame and spark.

'I bind thee, Jennet Scot, to this valley.' Ma threw a handful of salt into the fire, which burned green and blue.

'I bind thee, Jennet Scot, to this valley.' A handful of rosemary followed.

'I bind thee, Jennet Scot, to this valley.' Heather this time.

'Is that it?' Sue asked.

'Not nearly,' Ma replied. 'If we're lucky she won't have noticed yet.' She turned back to the fire. 'Throw in that stone.'

'What?'

'Thee heard me. Get it in the fire, quick.'

John did as he was told.

'I bind thee, Jennet Scot, to this hearthstone of Wolf Farm.' Salt.

'I bind thee, Jennet Scot, to this hearthstone of Wolf Farm.' Rosemary.

'I bind thee, Jennet Scot, to this hearthstone of Wolf Farm.' Heather.

Ma turned to John and Sue. 'Get it out of the fire. Use them tongs. And get it to the church, quick as thee likes. She won't notice, yet. This cottage means nowt to her, it's new. But she ain't daft, she'll work it out soon enough.'

John fished the stone out of the fire with the poker and tongs and it clanged on the hearth.

'Care, boy! Don't break it, this is our only chance.'

'Sorry, Ma.'

Sue passed him a folded towel and John lifted the stone and headed out the door.

'Go quickly, Son. Thee too, Sue. I'll distract her best I can.'

'I bloody well hope so,' John muttered.

*

'John, look how deep it is already.'

'I know.'

'How can we get this bloody great big stone out to the church by swimming? It'll drown us both.'

'Wait here.' John dashed off and returned ten minutes later dragging a small rowing boat along the edge of what was now most decidedly looking like a reservoir.

'Wilf's old fishing boat,' he said with a grin. 'The old bugger had me rescue it from the river and drag it up the bloody hill last month. Can't bear to see anything go to waste or be chucked out until there's nothing left of it to chuck. It should get us and the stone out there, at least.'

They heaved the stone into the bottom of the boat, then John held it steady while Sue climbed in. He pushed off and launched himself inside – a sprawl of legs and arms that she could not help laughing at despite the severity of the situation. Her laughter cut off at a vicious blast of lightning and thunder. 'That struck the bank – she only just missed us.'

'Bloody hell! She knows what we're doing – quick, get rowing, we haven't got much time. I hope to God Ma knows what *she's* doing.'

The boat bumped against the stone wall of the church and Sue only just managed to grab hold of a gargoyle on the roof edge to hold them in place.

'John, the door's underwater already – how are we going to get the stone inside?'

'I'll break a bloody hole in the roof if I have to,' he said. 'Richie's life depends on it. I won't lose another child to this bitch – however old or powerful she is.'

Sue said nothing, just held on tighter with gritted teeth.

John clambered on to the roof of the church. 'Pass me the stone.'

'How? I need both hands to hang on!'

'I'll hold on to the boat. Just put the stone on the roof.'

Sue let go, noticing John's knuckles turn white as he took the strain from his awkward position. She needed both hands and a knee to heave the hearthstone up, and as soon as she let go it started to slide.

'No!' they both cried, and John let go of the boat's gunwale to stop it slithering into the water.

'John!' Sue shouted and grabbed for the edge of the church roof. Her momentum forced the boat from under her and she splashed into the water, kicking hard to help herself gain purchase on the wet, slippery slate tiles. Lightning and thunder cracked overhead.

'Sue!'

'Get the stone inside, I'm okay.'

'No, grab my hand.'

'John, please, this could mean Richie's life.'

John said nothing, but turned himself around, his leg securing the stone. He began the laborious task of pushing it up the steep roof, but every inch he gained was immediately lost again. The roof was too wet, too mossy, and too steep. He had no choice but to begin prising away slate tiles where he was.

'They won't budge – they're fixed tight,' he called.

'Then smash them!' Sue had managed to get a leg on to the roof and hauled herself to safety.

'Grab hold of the stone and brace yourself, don't let it slip.'

She shuffled over and used her body as a brace between the stone and the gargoyle she'd anchored herself to earlier.

John sat back and used the heel of his boot to smash the roof tiles. When he had a hole large enough, he started to push the hearthstone towards the gap.

'John, no!'

'What?'

'Is the inside flooded?'

He peered through the hole. 'I don't think so, not yet – the water level's still low.'

'The stone can't break, it's our only chance. We need to wait until it's deep. Then it can sink and stay in one piece.'

John looked at her. 'You're right, but can we wait that long?' He glanced up as another flash of lightning lit them from above and cringed at the force of the thunder.

'We have to.'

Old Ma Ramsgill continued her chanting of, 'I bind thee, Jennet Scot, to this valley. Thee'll do no more harm here. I bind thee Jennet Scot—' She screamed as something knocked her down. Screamed again as her body broke. Then resumed her chant.

The storm above the valley intensified.

'Got thee now, bitch,' Ma whispered. 'Got thee on t' run – too busy celebrating thy freedom, forgot what was—' She screamed again as lightning struck nearby.

'Missed, bitch!' She cackled into the sudden dark as the lights went out. 'That all thee got? Terrorise my family, would thee? Ha!'

Another scream as her leg was twisted and she felt –

and heard – another bone break. 'Do what thee likes to me – I've lived a long life, more than thee ever did. Too late to stop me now!'

The fire flared and sparks leapt out into the room.

'No!' Old Ma Ramsgill screamed, louder than she had for sixty years. Sparks landed on the pile of journals and bred flames. As they took hold, Ma forced her broken body along the floor and reached out. She found her own journal, dragged it out of the inferno, beat it against the floor, then rolled on top of it to smother the flames. She passed out.

'John!' Sue screamed as lightning struck the steeple. 'Do it now – she's too strong.'

John glanced up at the sky then turned to Sue. 'I don't know if it's deep enough.'

'It has to be, just do it before she stops us.'

He nodded, once, then pushed the heavy stone towards the hole in the church roof.

Right at the edge he paused and looked at his wife. 'Are you sure?'

'Yes. Just do it.'

Lightning struck again, blinding them both.

As Sue's sight slowly came back, she searched for her husband. 'John? John? *John!*' The last word was a shriek. He had gone.

Sobbing, she pulled herself to the hole in the roof and peered down. All was black. She could see nothing.

Lightning flashed again and she had a split-second image of John's twisted body, floating face down in the water below.

'Nooo! You fucking bitch, Jennet, no!' She turned her face to the sky as distant thunder rumbled and the church bell pealed.

Another flash. John still didn't move. There was nothing she could do. She couldn't get to him and Richie needed a mother.

The bell continued to ring and she realised: it was Jennet. She'd claimed another victim, but the bell was the only way she could now express her fury.

The ringing faded. It was over. At least for now.

Soundlessly, Sue slid off the roof and into the water. She swam ashore, silent tears adding to the new Thruscross Reservoir. She was a widow but her son was safe. The only person left on this earth who carried Ramsgill blood.

16th August 1966 – 2:00 p.m.

'Here thee goes, Ma,' Wilf said, passing her a heavy carrier bag. 'Don't let the nurses see.'

Ma peered into the bag and grinned before pulling out one of many bottles of Oatmeal Stout. 'That's good of thee, this'll do a damn sight more good than them pills they keep making me take.'

'Don't be daft, Ma. Everyone knows what thee did – thee'll never have to pay for another drink in the Stonehouse, that's for damn certain.'

'Right, well give Sue one then and thee can bring some more tomorrow.'

Wilf chuckled as Sue walked back into the room and took the bottle Ma held out to her.

'Is it really over, Ma?'

'I bloody well hope so, lass. At least for now.'

'What do you mean? Will she be back?'

'She's always managed it in the past. Just promise me one thing.'

'What?'

'Don't drink the bloody tap water and don't let Richie have even a drop.'

'What?'

'That reservoir. It's to supply drinking water. Don't use the tap water and *never* let Richie – or his kids – drink it.'

Sue stared at her.

'Jennet's in there – in that water. She's bound to it. If even a drop of Thruscross water makes it into the glass of a Ramsgill, Jennet will gain strength. Maybe enough to come back.'

21st August 1966 – 2:00 p.m.

'Ey lass, thee's a good 'un to visit me every day as thee does.'

'Ma, Ma, Ma!'

Sue lifted Richie up on to Old Ma Ramsgill's hospital bed and he snuggled up to his grandmother.

'Did thee rescue any of the journals?' Ma asked once she'd hugged her grandson.

Sue shook her head. 'Only the one you saved. But rain stopped the house burning.'

Ma nodded. 'Keep that journal safe, and make sure thee passes it on to Richie and he knows to pass it on to his kids. There's a lot of stuff from the others in there. I hope I've copied all the important bits. Should have left the others at Gate House.'

'Ma, about Gate House . . .'

Old Ma Ramsgill looked up sharply at her daughter-in-law.

'It-it was struck by lightning. I'm sorry, it's gone. But you'll be all right, you'll stay with us.'

Ma said nothing, but her sorrow was clear on her face.

'There's something else. They're going to demolish the church,' Sue added quietly.

'What's that thee's saying?'

'Someone must have seen us that night on the church roof. They're concerned about people swimming out to it if they leave it. Part of the steeple was still above the water when the reservoir was full. Anyway, they've decided it's too much of a risk. When they let the water out, they'll take it apart and take all the internal fittings to that new monstrosity they've built on the other hill.'

'Buggertion.'

'Does that mean she'll be free again?'

'Don't know, lass. It'll still be holy ground, it depends on whether they move her stone. Did it go right to the bottom?'

'I don't know.'

'Then we can only hope, lass, nowt more we can do now. Pass me another of them stouts.'

The End

Book 3 in the Ghosts of Thores-Cross series,
***JENNET: now she wants the children*, is**
available now.

Reviews

If you enjoyed *Cursed*, please consider leaving a rating and review on Amazon. Reviews and feedback are incredibly important to an author, as well as potential readers, and are very much appreciated.

For more information on the full range of Karen Perkins' fiction, including links for the main retailer sites and details of her current writing projects, please go to Karen's website:
www.karenperkinsauthor.com/

Author's Note

Thruscross Reservoir does exist, and covers the drowned village of West End – one of a number of small hamlets that made up the parish of Thruscross – previously known as Thores-Cross. The dam was finished in 1966 and the test flood covered everything in the valley – except the top of the church. After a man was spotted sitting on the roof and swimming back to the shore, the church was demolished to prevent this happening again.

It must have seemed in 1966 that the village beneath Thruscross was gone for good, but it does rise now and then, whenever there's a drought severe enough to dry out the reservoir . . .

Acknowledgements

Thank you to Christina Robinson of Robinson Bobcat Hire for her expert tutelage about road building and the hazards – and inconveniences – encountered by those who keep us on the move.

Louise Burke, thank you for all your help and objectivity – it can't be easy to edit an editor; you do a wonderful job and save me much embarrassment.

Cecelia Morgan, what can I say? Your vision and quite simply amazing talent have once again created a wonderful cover. I am so proud to be working with you, and count myself blessed that *Cursed* carries your work.

Also thank you to the staff of the Rampsbeck Country House Hotel in Ullswater for looking after me so well – I wrote non-stop and the first draft of this tale was written in its entirety on the terrace.

Books by Karen Perkins

The Yorkshire Ghost Stories

Ghosts of Thores-Cross
The Haunting of Thores-Cross: A Yorkshire Ghost
Story
Cursed: A Yorkshire Ghost Short Story
JENNET: now she wants the children

Ghosts of Haworth
Parliament of Rooks: Haunting Brontë Country

Ghosts of Knaresborough
Knight of Betrayal: A Medieval Haunting

To find out more about the full range of Yorkshire
Ghost Stories, including upcoming titles, please visit:
www.karenperkinsauthor.com/yorkshire-ghosts

The Great Northern Witch Hunts

Murder by Witchcraft: A Pendle Witch Short Story
Divided by Witchcraft: Inspired by the true story of the
Samlesbury Witches

To find out more about the full range of books in the
Great Northern Witch Hunts series, please visit:
www.karenperkinsauthor.com/pendle-witches

*

The Valkyrie Series
Historical Caribbean Nautical Adventure

Look Sharpe! (Book #1)
Ill Wind (Book #2)
Dead Reckoning (Book #3)

The Valkyrie Series: The First Fleet (Look Sharpe!, Ill
Wind & Dead Reckoning)

To find out more about the full range of books in the
Valkyrie Series, please visit:
www.karenperkinsauthor.com/valkyrie

About the Author

Karen Perkins is the author of the Yorkshire Ghost Stories, the Pendle Witch Short Stories and the Valkyrie Series of historical nautical fiction. All of her fiction has appeared at the top of bestseller lists on both sides of the Atlantic, including the top 21 in the UK Kindle Store in 2018.

Her first Yorkshire Ghost Story – THE HAUNTING OF THORES-CROSS – won the Silver Medal for European Fiction in the prestigious 2015 Independent Publisher Book Awards in New York, whilst her Valkyrie novel, DEAD RECKONING, was long-listed in the 2011 MSLEXIA novel competition.

Originally a financial advisor, a sailing injury left Karen with a chronic pain condition which she has been battling for over twenty five years (although she did take the European ladies title despite the injury!). Writing has given her a new lease of – and purpose to – life, and she is currently working on *A Question of Witchcraft* – a sequel to *Parliament of Rooks: Haunting Brontë Country,* as well as more Pendle Witch short stories.

To find out more about current writing projects as well as special offers and competitions, you are very welcome to join Karen in her Facebook group. This is an exclusive group where you can get the news first, as well as have access to early previews and chances to get your hands on new books before anyone else. Find us on Facebook at:

www.facebook.com/groups/karenperkinsbookgroup

See more about Karen Perkins, including contact details and sign up to her newsletter, on her website:
www.karenperkinsauthor.com

Karen is on Social Media:

Facebook:
www.facebook.com/karenperkinsauthor
www.facebook.com/Yorkshireghosts
www.facebook.com/groups/karenperkinsbookgroup

Twitter:
@LionheartG

Instagram:
@yorkshireghosts

Excerpt from JENNET: now she wants the children

Prologue
Present Day

I'm tired. So, so tired. After such a long banishment from the physical world by those damnable villagers, I'm in the darkness again. It's been too long.

My babbies are here too – they've been here all this time, ever since, ever since ...

Nay, I can't think about that day, the one day I held them in my arms.

* * *

They're in the darkness somewhere: I can hear them, sense them, just out of reach. I can't fail them again, I can't. I have to get back. I have to give them life. Whatever it takes.

The last of them meddling women to best me, the one that married a Ramsgill, the awd carlin Ma, she's long in her grave now, and the flood rid the valley of the whole village.

The Ramsgills are all gone. There's none left – none strong enough to fight me again. This time I will succeed. This time I will birth my babbies. Little Charlie and Allie.

* * *

'Well, we've done it,' Paul Wainwright said. 'Moved back home, as near as damn it. The kids'll grow up in the same landscape their ancestors helped to form.'

Ruth bent to unclip Betsy's lead, then leaned into her husband and his encircling arm as the Yorkshire terrier dashed off after the children.

'I hope we've done the right thing,' Ruth said. 'It doesn't quite feel right to be living in that house after what happened to them all.'

'I know, but life goes on, and Sammy and Clare can grow up here, instead of on a housing estate somewhere in town.'

Ruth sighed. Paul stopped, turned and peered at his diminutive wife. She stood five feet tall and barely reached his chest, and he held back a grin at the extent to which she had to crane her head to meet his gaze.

'What happened was a tragedy. Pure and simple. An accident. Anyroad, the new house is very different, we've made it our own. We're lucky to have it – we'd never have been able to live out here if it hadn't been passed down to you.'

'Good old Great-Aunt Ma Ramsgill. Great-great-aunt,' Ruth corrected herself. 'I can still remember her, clear as day – she was over a hundred when she died, and no one was surprised when she got her telegram from the Queen.'

'Got a surprise when she bought everyone a glass of stout at the Stone House, though – even us kids!' Paul said with a laugh, and resumed walking, his arm around his wife's shoulders. Holding hands wasn't an option for them.

'Ha, that's right,' Ruth said. 'She swore the stout was what kept her going for so long.'

'I wonder where the Wainwright house was?' Paul said as they emerged from the trees and paused at the edge of what was supposed to be a reservoir.

* * *

It's becoming harder to keep my will in this void. I can feel my energy sapping, the forces here taking from me.

My babbies are holding on, and so can I.

I must.

I cannot fail. Not this time.

* * *

A dry winter had been followed by a sunny spring, and May had witnessed the water level drop to almost nothing. The village had surfaced once more.

'Be careful, you two!' Ruth called to the children, Sammy and Clare. Excited squeals told the adults that the hard, cracked earth they were standing on, transformed to soft, deep peaty mud just a few yards away.

Clare sank up to her knees and cried out for help. At eight, Sammy took his big-brother duties to heart. He told Clare to stand in his footprints.

'Slow down, slow down,' Clare called. 'Let me hold on to you.'

Sammy did as he was bid, and neither child noticed Betsy's startled reaction to the soft ground. Nor her desperate – and filthy – struggle back to firmer footing.

Paul took pity on the shaking dog and picked her up, ignoring Ruth's protest as his T-shirt was muddied by Betsy's frantic paws. He soothed their pet, calming her, and she soon looked quite content in her safe, lofty perch.

Paul batted Ruth's hand away as she flapped at the mud on his clothing. 'There's no point fussing about that. Don't you remember the last time Thruscross dried up in the nineties? We played down here when we weren't much older than them two. I was so covered in mud, my parents stripped me then hosed me off before they let me in the house.'

'Hmm,' Ruth said. 'I think mine did the same.'

She stepped forward, her wellington boot sinking further as she watched. She tried to pull her foot up, but the sucking mud would not release its prize, and she fell backwards, leaving the boot behind, her socked foot waving in the air.

Paul offered her a hand, his mirth escaping despite his best efforts to suppress it. 'Shall I carry you as well?'

Ruth scowled at him. 'It's not fair, your legs are twice the length of mine.' She squealed as Paul hauled her upright. She wobbled, but her grip on Paul's hand was not enough to steady her and she had no option but to put her bootless foot down to find her balance.

She stared down at herself, sighed and bent to roll up her jeans legs, then removed her socks and remaining boot. She couldn't pull her lost one out of the mud, so stood, hands on hips, and blew upwards at the muddy blonde hair stuck to her forehead, muttering, 'Why didn't I just wear shorts?'

'Sammy, Sammy, look, Mummy's the Abomble Mudman!'

'Abominable,' Sammy corrected.

'That's what I said, abomble.' Clare mimicked her mother's stance, and Paul's laughter filled the valley.

JENNET: now she wants the children
is available now

Printed in Great Britain
by Amazon